**Dear Parents,**

Congratulations! Your child has embarked on an exciting journey – they're learning to read! As a parent, you can be there to support and cheer them along as they take their first steps.

At school, children are taught how to decode words and arrange these building blocks of language into sentences and wonderful stories.

At home, parents play a vital part in reinforcing these new-found skills. You can help your child practise their reading by providing well-written, engaging stories, which you can enjoy together.

This series – **Ready, Steady, Read!** – offers exactly that, and more. These stories support inexperienced readers by:

- gradually introducing new vocabulary
- using repetition to consolidate learning
- gradually increasing sentence length and word count
- providing texts that boost a young reader's confidence.

As each book is completed, engaging activities encourage young readers to look back at the story, while a Picture Dictionary reinforces new vocabulary. Enjoyment is the key – and reading together can be great fun for both parent and child!

**Prue Goodwin**
Lecturer in Literacy and Children's Books

The **Ready, Steady, Read!** series has 4 levels. The facing page shows what you can expect to find in the books at each level.

As your child's confidence grows, they can progress to books from the higher levels. These will keep them engaged and encourage new reading skills.

The levels are only meant as guides; together, you and your child can pick the book that will be just right.

Here are some handy tips for helping children who are ready for reading!

**Give them choice** – Letting children pick a book (from the level that's right for them) makes them feel involved.

**Talk about it** – Discussing the story and the pictures helps children engage with the book.

**Read it again** – Repetition of favourite stories reinforces learning.

**Cheer them on!** – Praise and encouragement builds a child's confidence and the belief in their growing ability.

## LEVEL **1** For first readers

* short, straightforward sentences
* basic, fun vocabulary
* simple, easy-to-follow stories of up to 100 words
* large print and easy-to-read design

## LEVEL **2** For developing readers

* longer sentences
* simple vocabulary, introducing new words
* longer stories of up to 200 words
* bold design, to capture readers' interest

## LEVEL **3** For more confident readers

* longer sentences with varied structure
* wider vocabulary
* high-interest stories of up to 300 words
* smaller print for experienced readers

## LEVEL **4** For able readers

* longer sentences with complex structure
* rich, exciting vocabulary
* complex stories of up to 400 words
* emphasis on text more than illustrations

Once you have read the story, you will find some amazing activities at the back of the book! There are Excellent Exercises for you to complete, plus a super Picture Dictionary.

But first it is time for the story . . .

# Ready?

# Steady?

# Let's read!

David Bedford    Elaine Field

# My Turn!

LITTLE TIGER PRESS
London

Oscar and Tilly were
at the playground.
"I am going on the
slide," said Tilly.

Playground

"My turn!" said Oscar.
"Not yet," said Tilly.

Then Tilly went on
the roundabout.
"My turn!" said Oscar.
"No, it is not!" said Tilly.

Tilly went round . . .
and ROUND . . .

"Now it *is* my turn," cried
Oscar. "*You* are too dizzy!"

"I feel better," said Tilly . . .

"Can I go on the swing?"
"Not yet," said Oscar.

"*My* turn on the see-saw!"
shouted Oscar.
But when he jumped on . . .

...Tilly went up!

# Then Tilly went down . . .

And Oscar went up!

After that . . .

Wheee!

Whooo!

Oscar and Tilly played
together all afternoon.

## Have you read the story? Well done!
## Now it is time for more fun!

Here are some questions about the story. Ask an adult to listen to your answers, and help if you get stuck.

## Take Turns

When Oscar and Tilly go the playground, they find it hard to take turns. Is there anything that *you* find hard to do?

## Perfect Playground

Can you name some of the things in this picture? What do *you* like to go on at the playground?

## Silly Tilly

Now describe what Tilly is doing in this picture.

## Fun Time

Can you remember how Oscar and Tilly spend the afternoon? What do *you* like to do in the afternoon?

Can you read all of these words from the story?

dizzy

jumped

Oscar

playground

roundabout

## see-saw

## slide

## swing

## Tilly

## together

Can you think of any other words that describe these pictures – for example, what colours can you see? Why not try to spell some of these words? Ask an adult to help!

## Can't You Sleep, Dotty?

Dotty has tried everything. But she just cannot sleep. Soon all her friends are trying to help her. But will anything work . . . ?

## Fred

Fred has a new little door. It's called a cat flap. But Fred knows that Horrible Henry is waiting outside, ready to pounce . . . !

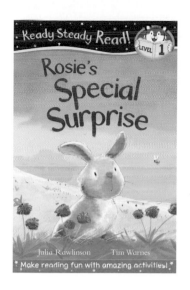

## Rosie's Special Surprise

Nosy Rosie likes to know everything about everything. So when Daddy Rabbit says he has a special surprise, she hops off to look for it. Whatever could it be?

## What Bear Likes Best!

Bear really likes to have fun. But all of his friends are busy and he keeps getting in the way! Will it ever be time to play?

*For Deborah — D B*
*For Maddy — E F*

LITTLE TIGER PRESS, 1 The Coda Centre, 189 Munster Road, London SW6 6AW
First published in Great Britain 2000
This edition published 2013
Text copyright © David Bedford 2000, 2013
Illustrations copyright © Elaine Field 2000, 2013
All rights reserved
Printed in China
978-1-84895 665-0
LTP/1800/0586/0413
2 4 6 8 10 9 7 5 3 1

# Books in the Series

## LEVEL 1 - For first readers

Can't You Sleep, Dotty?

Fred

My Turn!

Rosie's Special Surprise

What Bear Likes Best!

## LEVEL 2 - For developing readers

Hopping Mad!

Newton

Ouch!

Where There's a Bear, There's Trouble!

The Wish Cat

## LEVEL 3 - For more confident readers

Lazy Ozzie

Little Mouse and the Big Red Apple

Nobody Laughs at a Lion!

Ridiculous!

Who's Been Eating My Porridge?

## LEVEL 4 - For able readers

The Biggest Baddest Wolf

Meggie Moon

Mouse, Mole and the Falling Star

The Nutty Nut Chase

Robot Dog